GW01087003

A story for every child who loves dinosaurs

Priya loved playing
with dinosaur toys
but someone at school
said they were for boys

Was it really true?
Priya thought to herself
as she put her favourite dino
back up on the shelf

Sighing with sadness
"I should get to bed
I'll dream about dino land
and adventures in my head"

When Priya was asleep
there was a burst of light
her toy began to sparkle
with the magic of the night

"Hello Priya
you sleepy head
time to wake up
and jump out of bed"

When Priya awoke
and opened her eyes
she couldn't believe it
her toy was ALIVE!

"Dina the Dino
you've grown so big
the size of a tree
instead of a twig!"

"It's dino magic
I'll explain on the way
we need your help
to save the day"

"Weeeee"

"Slide down my neck
adventures await
hold on tight
we don't want to be late"

"We need a hero
just like you
with strength, smarts
and bravery too"

Off they flew
into the night
stars around them
shining bright

Clouds of magic
began to appear
DINO LAND
was getting near

They flew through the clouds
their feet touched the ground
where three more dinos
were standing around

"A storm blocked our stream
we've tried all we can
but we're out of ideas
can you think of a plan?"

Priya turned to the dinos
"Don't you realise I'm small
How can I help
when I'm not even tall?"
"Priya don't you see
it's not about your height
you just need to believe
with all of your might"
"If you need a little help
take this magic mask
it will give you the courage
to finish the task"

Dina and Priya
held onto the log
got ready to push
and clear the clog

They pushed and they pulled
but the dam wouldn't budge
not even a smidgen
not even a nudge ...

She couldn't give up
her friends were in need
so Priya got back up
to complete the deed

"Listen up dinos
and follow my rules
we'll need to work together
and find a few tools"

"Dina find some vines
your neck is the longest
Sammy break some branches
your horn is the strongest

"Terry hold a rock
in the HUGE jaw you've got
drop it when I count
to get the perfect shot"

The catapult was built
with each giving a hand
now for the final step
of the winning plan

Working together
and using their skills
they catapulted the logs
as far as the hills
3... 2... 1...

With the logs now gone
the stream poured down
dinos jumped in
splashing around

"You did it Priya
you saved the day
we knew you could
HIP HIP HOORAY!"

"We better get you home
before the morning light
when I turn back into a toy
without the magic of the night

You'll see me again
more adventures await
more fun to be had
and memories to make"

Snuggled up tight
with Dina back as a toy
Priya now knew for sure
dinos weren't just for boys

Dinos had taught Priya ...
Strength can mean muscles
but it can also mean smarts
and ANYTHING is possible
when you believe with your heart

MAKE YOUR OWN MAGIC MASK

DESIGN YOUR OWN MAGIC MASK

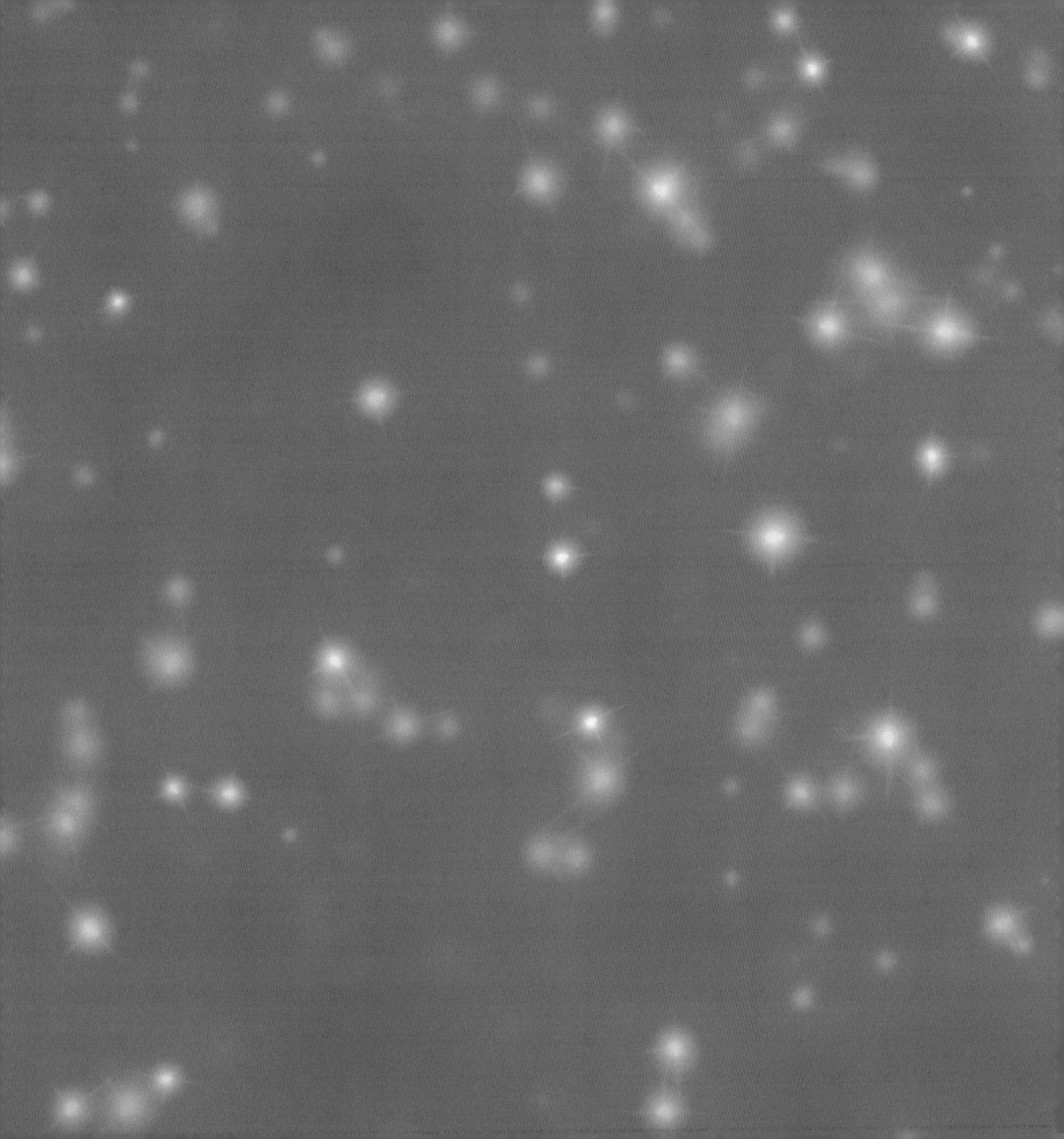

Printed in Great Britain
by Amazon

24123823R00023